# THE TWO MOUNTAINS
## AN AZTEC LEGEND

RETOLD BY Eric A. Kimmel
ILLUSTRATED BY Leonard Everett Fisher

HOLIDAY HOUSE / NEW YORK

To Leonard
*E. A. K.*

To Eric
*L. E. F.*

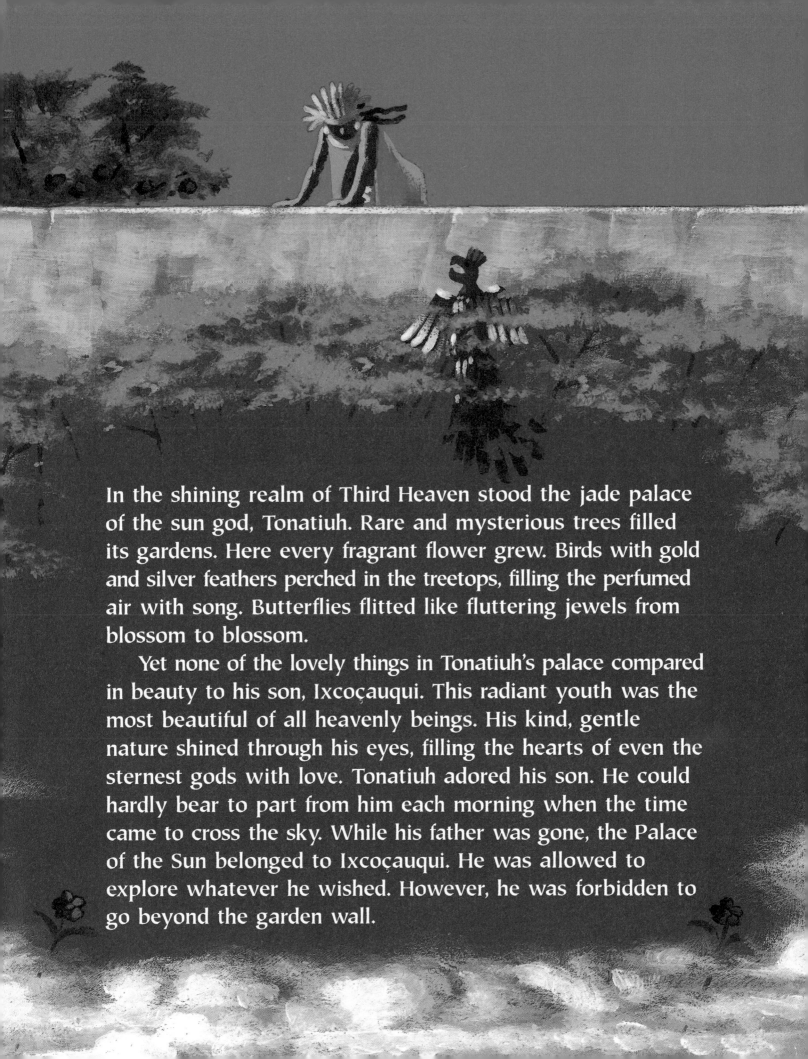

In the shining realm of Third Heaven stood the jade palace of the sun god, Tonatiuh. Rare and mysterious trees filled its gardens. Here every fragrant flower grew. Birds with gold and silver feathers perched in the treetops, filling the perfumed air with song. Butterflies flitted like fluttering jewels from blossom to blossom.

Yet none of the lovely things in Tonatiuh's palace compared in beauty to his son, Ixcoçauqui. This radiant youth was the most beautiful of all heavenly beings. His kind, gentle nature shined through his eyes, filling the hearts of even the sternest gods with love. Tonatiuh adored his son. He could hardly bear to part from him each morning when the time came to cross the sky. While his father was gone, the Palace of the Sun belonged to Ixcoçauqui. He was allowed to explore whatever he wished. However, he was forbidden to go beyond the garden wall.

One evening Ixcoçauqui asked his father, "Why may I never go beyond the garden?"

"I worry when you are out of my sight," Tonatiuh said. "I fear you may encounter some danger."

"Why should you be afraid, Father?" Ixcoçauqui asked. "Am I not a god? Nothing in the heavens or on earth can harm me."

Tonatiuh replied, "I am your father. If I forbid you to go beyond the garden wall, you must obey."

Ixcoçauqui nodded, but he did not answer. He thought to himself, There must be something beyond the garden that my father does not want me to see. He became more determined than ever to learn what it was.

At dawn the next morning, when Tonatiuh set out on his daily journey across the sky, Ixcoçauqui slipped over the garden wall. He followed a trail through a deep forest. It led to the shores of a clear blue lake. A maiden sat beside its waters, combing her hair. As he approached, she spoke to him.

"Ixcoçauqui! Has your father allowed you to leave his garden?"

"He would never allow me to do that," Ixcoçauqui replied. "I climbed the wall without his permission. Had I known you were here, I would have left the garden long ago. No goddess in the thirteen heavens is as beautiful as you. I beg you, tell me your name."

The maiden answered, "My name is Coyolxauhqui. I am the daughter of Mixtli, goddess of the moon."

Ixcoçauqui sat down beside her. They spent the rest of the afternoon together. By the end of the day the young couple had fallen in love.

"I must return home before my father arrives," Ixcoçauqui said as the shadows deepened.

"And I must go back to my mother. Will we meet again?" Coyolxauhqui asked.

"Soon," Ixcoçauqui promised.

The two lovers continued meeting secretly by the lake, among the stars and planets, in the hidden corners of the thirteen heavens. Their love grew so deep that they could not bear to be apart. Ixcoçauqui asked his father to allow them to be married.

"When did you meet Mixtli's daughter?" Tonatiuh shouted.

"I climbed over the garden wall without your permission," Ixcoçauqui confessed. "We met by the lake. Since then we have fallen in love. I am sorry I disobeyed, Father, but it is done. Do not deny us our happiness now."

"Disobedience must be punished," Tonatiuh said. "I will never allow you to be married. All the other gods will agree with me."

The gods held a council to decide what to do. Tonatiuh opposed the marriage. Mixtli favored it. Coyolxauhqui and Ixcoçauqui begged the gods to consider their happiness. In the end, the gods agreed.

"These two young people have fallen in love. They ask for our blessing. Let us not withhold it, lest their love turn to bitterness."

So Coyolxauhqui and Ixcoçauqui were married. All the gods in the thirteen heavens took part in the celebration. Except Tonatiuh. As much as he loved his son, he could not forgive him for opposing his wishes.

"I will bless your wedding on one condition," Tonatiuh said. "You both must promise never to leave the heavens. Should you attempt to visit the earth without my permission, you will face severe punishment. You will be gods no longer."

"Why are you so harsh?" Mixtli asked Tonatiuh. "Why can't our children visit the earth whenever they wish? Gods and goddesses go there all the time."

"My son must learn to obey. If he wishes me to bless his wedding, he must do as I demand."

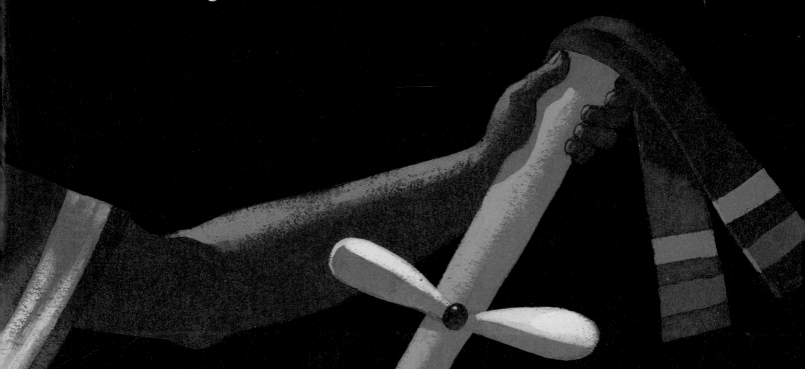

Coyolxauhqui and Ixcoçauqui wanted peace in their family. They agreed to swear as Tonatiuh wished. Mictlantecuhtli, lord of the dead, witnessed their vow and sealed it forever. This vow could never be taken back or changed.

Coyolxauhqui and Ixcoçauqui began their lives together. Each day was filled with happiness. But after a time Ixcoçauqui began to wonder, "I have never been to earth. There must be something down there that my father doesn't want me to know about. What could it be?"

Coyolxauhqui agreed. "It must be beautiful and rare. Perhaps we should find out what it is. If you had obeyed your father and stayed behind the garden wall, we never would have met."

The more they thought about earth and its mysteries, the more they became intrigued. "Let us go down to the lowest heaven. We can look at the earth from there without breaking our vow."

Coyolxauhqui and Ixcoçauqui descended to First Heaven, the realm of the clouds, which is closest to earth. Looking below, they saw a beautiful valley filled with sparkling lakes, broad meadows, and deep, mysterious forests. The longer they looked, the more entranced they became.

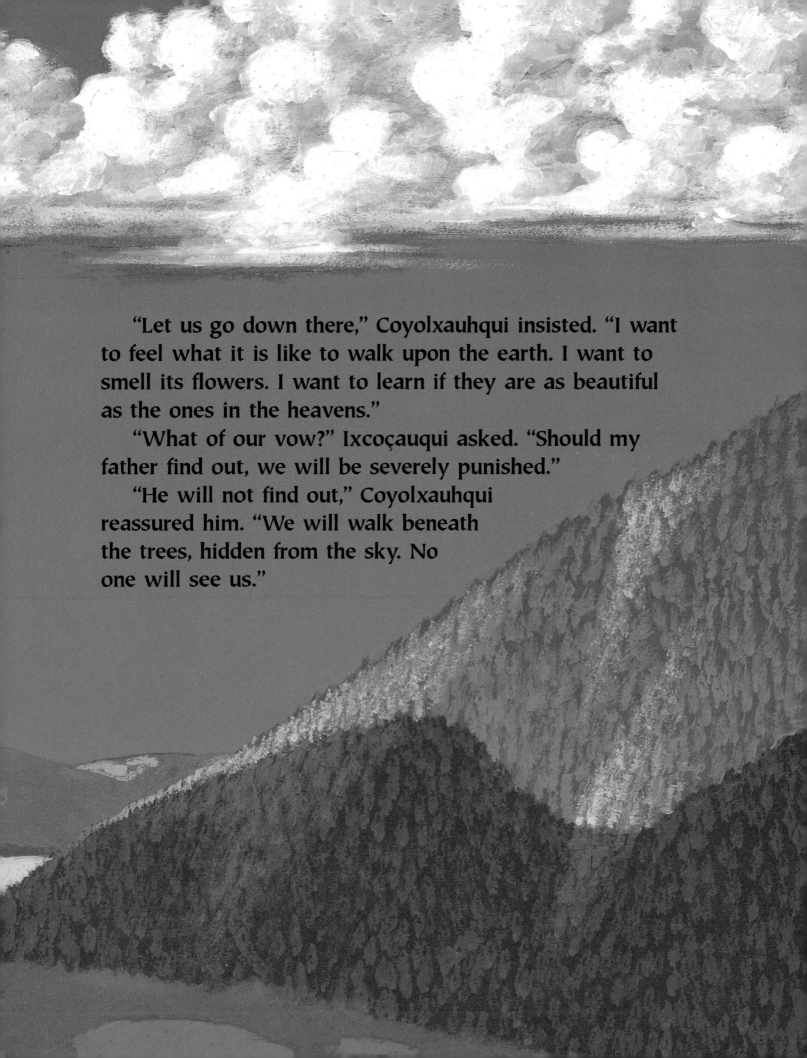

"Let us go down there," Coyolxauhqui insisted. "I want to feel what it is like to walk upon the earth. I want to smell its flowers. I want to learn if they are as beautiful as the ones in the heavens."

"What of our vow?" Ixcoçauqui asked. "Should my father find out, we will be severely punished."

"He will not find out," Coyolxauhqui reassured him. "We will walk beneath the trees, hidden from the sky. No one will see us."

The young couple descended to earth. They bathed in quiet pools. They walked through forest shadows. They marveled at the flowers and birds they encountered, finding in them a rare beauty.

"Everything lives forever in the realm of the gods," Coyolxauhqui said. "These things of earth only last for a few brief moments. They wither, die, and fade away. That makes them even more precious."

Ixcoçauqui agreed. "As I walk on earth, I feel that time is passing. I never thought about time in the heavens."

Ixcoçauqui and Coyolxauhqui returned to earth again and again. One day Hummingbird saw them walking through the forest. She flew to First Heaven and said to Tlaloc, the rain god, "Why are the children of the sun and moon walking on earth?"

Their secret had been revealed. Ixcoçauqui and Coyolxauhqui had broken their oath. Now they faced certain punishment.

Tonatiuh pleaded with the lord of death. "I only wanted to frighten my son so that he would never disobey me again. I did not think he would ever break his vow. The punishment is too severe. It must be changed."

But Mictlantecuhtli remained unmoved. "Once an oath is sworn and sealed, it can never be altered. It remains fixed until the end of time."

Ixcoçauqui and Coyolxauhqui would be gods no more. They were banished from the heavens. From now on they would live on earth as mortals. They would work from sunrise to sunset to provide the food they ate. They would endure hunger and thirst. The sun would burn their bodies; the wind would chill their bones. They would suffer sickness and sorrow, and at the end of their lives, death.

"It does not matter," said Ixcoçauqui to Coyolxauhqui. "I can bear any punishment if we are together. Earth has its own beauty. We will make a place for ourselves there."

The young couple had to learn many skills. They had to work hard to grow food, make clothing, and build shelter. But they also took pride in what they learned and in the work they accomplished. They experienced joy in making plants grow and in harvesting their fruits. At evening, when the work of the day was done, they sang and danced together.

One morning Coyolxauhqui could not rise from her mat. "What is wrong?" Ixcoçauqui asked.

"I do not know. I have never felt this way before. My head hurts. My arms and legs feel weak."

"You are sick," Ixcoçauqui told her. "Do not worry. There are healing plants in the forest. I have watched animals eat them and get better. I will gather some for you."

Ixcoçauqui brewed teas of healing plants for Coyolxauhqui. He experimented with different roots and leaves. Nothing helped. Coyolxauhqui grew weaker every day. Finally she said, "I feel my life is ending. This must be what mortals call death."

"Now I know what sorrow means. Is there nothing I can do?" Ixcoçauqui asked, tears running from his eyes.

"Carry me to the top of that mountain," Coyolxauhqui murmured. "I will be close to First Heaven, my mother's realm. She can kiss me farewell as she passes across the night sky."

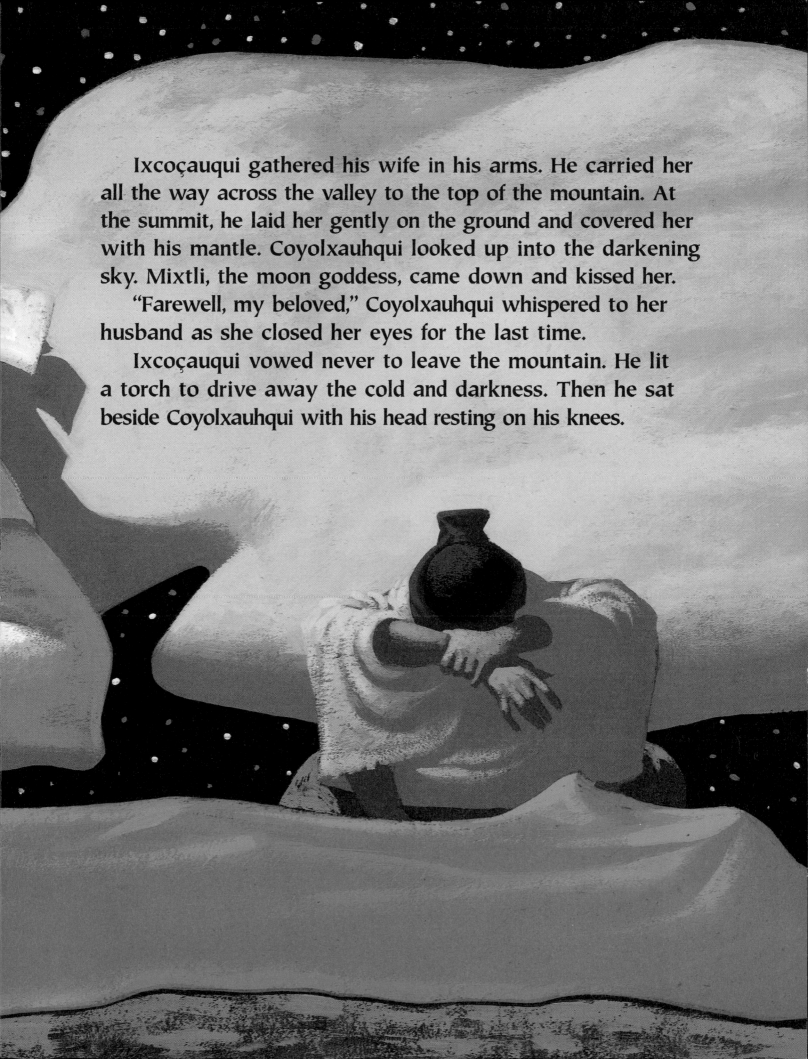

Ixcoçauqui gathered his wife in his arms. He carried her all the way across the valley to the top of the mountain. At the summit, he laid her gently on the ground and covered her with his mantle. Coyolxauhqui looked up into the darkening sky. Mixtli, the moon goddess, came down and kissed her.

"Farewell, my beloved," Coyolxauhqui whispered to her husband as she closed her eyes for the last time.

Ixcoçauqui vowed never to leave the mountain. He lit a torch to drive away the cold and darkness. Then he sat beside Coyolxauhqui with his head resting on his knees.

The gods looked down in sorrow. Mixtli and Tonatiuh wept hardest of all.

"Let our children be together as long as the earth endures," they said.

The gods transformed the two young lovers into two mountains overlooking the Valley of Mexico. Coyolxauhqui is known as *Iztaccihuatl*, which means "the Lady of the Snows." Seen from afar, she resembles a sleeping woman. A snowy mantle covers her in all seasons.

Ixcoçauqui rests nearby. He is called *Popocatepetl* or "Smoking Hill." A plume of volcanic smoke rises from the mountain's peak, calling to mind Ixcoçauqui's fiery torch. From time to time the mountain rumbles and groans. People feel the earth tremble. Then they say to each other, "It is Ixcoçauqui, mourning for his beloved."

# AUTHOR'S NOTE

The Valley of Mexico is geologically active. The people who live there have many stories about the region's volcanoes. *The Two Mountains* is a legend of the Nahua people, the modern descendants of the Aztecs. My source for the story was "La Leyenda de los Volcanes" in Otilia Meza's *Leyendas Prehispanicas Mexicanas* (Panorama Editorial, 1990).

## PRONUNCIATION GUIDE

| | |
|---|---|
| Tonatiuh | (toe-nah-TI-yuh) |
| Ixcoçauqui | (eetz-co-TZAU-key) |
| Coyolxauhqui | (coy-ol-SHAU-key) |
| Mixtli | (MEESH-tlee) |
| Mictlantecuhtli | (meeck-tlan-tay-KOO-tlee) |
| Tlaloc | (TLAH-lok) |
| Iztaccihuatl | (eez-tahk-SEE-wahtl) |
| Popocatepetl | (po-po-ka-TAY-petl) |

The author wishes to thank Geoff and Sharisse McCafferty, Assistant Professors of Archaeology at the University of Calgary, for their help with Nahuatl spelling and pronunciation.

Text copyright © 2000 by Eric A. Kimmel
Illustrations copyright © 2000 by Leonard Everett Fisher
All Rights Reserved
Printed in the United States of America
First Edition
The text typeface is Tiepolo Bold.
The illustrations for this book were created
in acrylic paint on paper.

Library of Congress Cataloging-in-Publication Data
Kimmel, Eric A.
The two mountains: an Aztec legend/by Eric A. Kimmel;
illustrated by Leonard Everett Fisher.—1st ed.
p. cm.
Summary: Two married gods disobey their orders and visit Earth, are
turned into mortals as punishment, and eventually become
mountains so that they will always stand side by side.
ISBN 0-8234-1504-X
1. Aztec mythology Juvenile literature. 2. Mountains—Mexico Folklore.
3. Volcanoes—Mexico Folklore. 4. Legends—Mexico. 5. Aztecs Folklore.
[1. Aztecs Folklore. 2. Indians of Mexico Folklore. 3. Folklore—Mexico.]
I. Fisher, Leonard Everett, ill. II. Title.
F1219.76.R45K56 2000
398.2'089'97452072—dc21
99-32881 CIP